A Few Sharp Sticks

A Few Sharp Sticks

An Informal Novel by

Brian Dedora

THE MERCURY PRESS & TEKSTEDITIONS

Teksteditions

Thanks also to the OAC's Arts Investment Fund.

The publisher gratefully acknowledges the financial assistance of the Canada Council for the Arts, the Ontario Arts Council, the Ontario Media Development Corporation, and the Ontario Book Publishing Tax Credit Program. The publisher further acknowledges the financial support of the Government of Canada through the Department of Canadian Heritage's Book Publishing Industry Development Program (BPIDP) for our publishing activities.

  Canada

Canada Council
for the Arts

Conseil des Arts
du Canada

Cover art: *Spurs*, acrylic on canvas, 2011, 60.5 x 47 cm, by Jonathan Syme
Cover art photographed by Ted Clark
Author photo: Delainy Mackie

Editor: Beverley Daurio
Composition and page design: Beverley Daurio

Canadian Cataloguing in Publication:
Dedora, Brian, 1946-
A few sharp sticks / Brian Dedora.

Also issued in electronic format.
ISBN 978-0-9868696-6-2
I. Title.
PS8557.E28F49 2011   C811'.54   C2011-901675-3

PRINT EDITION ISBN 978-1-55128-153-7

The Mercury Press
www.themercurypress.ca
&
Teksteditions
www.teksteditions.com

A Few Sharp Sticks

A.

He distinguishes friendships out of a common pursuit; some last for a while and come under social relations   or group relations but always relations of intervention...

probe a psychic wound beyond an intermeddling thrust into the concerns of others from idle but officious curiosity; a stepping-in on behalf of the weaker to plead argumentative appeal to feeling, under the influence of motives all the way from cold self-interest to noble impulses with intense, impassioned earnestness of personal considerations, whereas solicit is a weak attempt to secure consent, sometimes by sordid or corrupt motives...

let me show you, beginning with the preposition *to* onwards to its end: the sibilant *s* runs into the hard *c* and lets go with *ure, u- r- e, secure* but then again runs into a hard *c* and is freed by the *s* before the *nt* of *n-t, consent* finishing at the comma but setting up for the *s&t* combo to follow in *sometimes* the *s&t* (familiar by now) introduces *m* plus *s* to run into the softer wall of *by* leading into the mainstay of the line after all that set up: follow the *o-r*, *sor or cor* followed by another *r* the double *rr* rupturing the word in two, for emphasis, but clipped by the impossible tightness of *p-t* as it

staggers the tongue as to where to go with it,
the *p* or *t* and end up with *corrupta* that slight
extra exhalation easing into the *m-o* stopped
at *t* and slid into the *v* of *motive* which can go
either way, hard or soft... *to secure consent,
sometimes by sordid or corrupt motives.*

so they would have you believe (let me be per-
fectly clear about the way I'm using "they":
it's not some 60s industrial military complex,
although they're a part of it, the whole... "they"
as us, all of us but with such mass isolation all
the rest of us becomes "they" when we are
alone and up against it when we need an intervention). So, what I said was...

"You don't feel you've crossed some line, but
you've crossed in some shifting sand some
drawn line aware only as you rubbed up against
the wall constructed on the shifting line where
you drew back in the face of direct questions
of continual presentations - tedium of heterosexual mechanisms... where after facing in-
surmountable odds veritable cliff-hangers

the guy, *deus ex machina*   (mere technology)
gets away with the girl

again

the whole dry popcorn of this engineering of
separation

i pod
u pod
we all pod Post-plod
to pay for our talking
our talking…

"take a look at the demographics
we'll see what our natures see

look!   the hero dresses to the left
as he walks down the long hall
there!   when he picks up the body
the outline of his briefs
under his tight flannels

What, you don't like fag money?

put it in
keep the money shot
make us happy"

a.

So much depends on speed time and distance,
any one unknown can be found if you have
two of three plus a rhumb line where east is
least and west is best with a variance of degrees
from true and with this dead reckoning, head
in a known direction straight into your wallet
without landfall ambiguity because we've plot-
ted your demographic profile...

So what we can do is this: we don't follow *abc*,
we cut it up so it's *cxm* with a subplot of *j* and
l... we can keep them on their toes, keep up
the interest with action and bring it together
at the very end where the jumble then becomes
abc all over again when he gets the girl, call it
artful... we can charge more.

B.

Justification of why in terms of human association imposed upon them of one type: unions.
This is, of course, regulation in light of pre-
formed patterns, patterns of indebtedness,
paternal & maternal.

a bringing together of distinct things to com-
bine, coalesce, form a new whole of things
brought together, never lost sight of, a fractured
bone or hearts in a marriage which cannot be
conceived of as resolved into parts even if con-
spicuously made up of parts, when a single
purpose, even better, an ideal so subserved by
all, that their possible separateness is lost sight
of despite the unity of the human body (that
particular oneness of volition) while what is
argued from the Right over Rite is a *homo*
nym.

b.

When he was getting a laying on of the hands, being strong-armed and almost lifted off his feet, along with some hard talk, I'd stand out of Our Father's vision but in my brother's view and wipe my finger off at him or stick out my tongue so he'd laugh and get hit harder...

if you were quick and smart, while you were laid over a footstool with your pants pulled down, you'd start wailing with tears to give the impression of really hurting to get him to relent, but also to disguise even more laughter at how pathetic this was, to get a look at your ass...

C.

Our experience of reality should make us sensitive   a very special interest of behaving homosexually and never giving it a thought; private associations he chooses to like.

Usually with serious aim, open to all of similar interests, especially of needs closely knit, whose members take an active part, usually social, membership obtained not by invitation or election but birth with its own quarters for meeting, recreation... a club of pleasure-seekers, a community of shakers, a company of friends... the whole body, one of their locals, a lodge, a bar, a steam bath, a club.

At last and alone and on my own at the junction of Yonge & Bloor. Look! Over there, across the street, it's Fred Davis looking debonair and polished just like on TV... walking down Yonge from Lonsdale to meet friends on Elm Street at a Balkan restaurant, Sue and Wendy, we'd been at Uvic together, even lived with Sue in a commune on Ludgate Street with Liz, Diane, and Ian... it's good to see them and we set up, over a dinner I've never had with tastes I'd never had and it tastes all right and I feel like I've arrived here in the city, to make it on my own: a typewriter, a bag of books, two changes of clothes and two hundred bucks... Sue was here to set me up with Wendy who had space over on Wellesley at Bleeker. We'd agreed that I'd stay at Lonsdale for another night and then move into Wendy's with my own space for fifty a month. I took plain old ice cream for dessert and was very happy. I'm on my own at last... I can come and go and with my own money do what I want and I had skills. We laughed and window shopped up Yonge; Wendy was in English and Drama, she would stage manage with a quart of coffee in a big black mug, a cigarette hanging at the side of her mouth... the last time I saw her, the locality of our lives took us apart, she was working for a lung cancer society and chided me on my smoking...

As we walked up Yonge, there! On the second floor at the corner the male symbol of two joined circles with pointed arrows... a gay bar... on my own, finally free, and I've just found my not so clean well-lighted place where I'll learn how to negotiate a roomful of men all wanting the same thing but not necessarily each other...

I saw Fred Davis today... right there, on the corner, I loved *Front Page Challenge*, there was old Gordon Sinclair playing up the Scots thrifty business by asking "How much do you make?" An appalling and never asked question in the tight WASP circles of the time. While beside him the fabulously dressed Betty

Kennedy would stutter a laugh which she passed to Pierre Berton and sometimes a guest panellist, all of this hosted and moderated by a polished Fred Davis who had all these voices for whatever came up on the show, being it was live. Smoothly moving from host in welcoming to moderating in a firmer tone or later when the challenger is asked questions by the panel, Fred could move in to open or close, remaining debonair... I saw Fred Davis today! The light of that programme all the way from Toronto, its big-city sophistication with people who made headlines...

Unlike Sunday night in the family room wading upstream through the corn syrup of *Father Knows Best*...

c.

Alarm at 6... whap it off and *move it* for the
shit shave shower shampoo... grab my clothes
dumped on the floor... head to the bathroom
dropping the clothes outside the door so I
won't splash them and sit... put the plug in
the sink and turn on the tap while I crap...
test the water with my left hand so the paper
won't stick... finish the wipe and turn off the
tap... out with the shaving gear... wet my
face... goop up the cream... lather it on and
swipe shave while I trace the day's critical path
to insert the cash jobs around the account
jobs... three days to pay day and counting...
I'm short a couple of grand... *move it*... rinse
off and pull the plug... turn on the shower...
test it... in quick... soap up shampoo and
rinse... grab the towel closest to the shower so
I don't have to go out into the colder air... do
the rub with a fast look in the mirror... thin
with no sags... on with the pit juice in with a
vitamin... clothes... undies socks shirt pants
sweater... *move*... shoes first coat last my briefcase and keys... lock the door and down to
the garage... unlock the car... I hate the
cold... start... put on the early morning jazz
station roar around the garage bang the bleeper
for the garage door wait for the green and gun
it out onto the street... hang a left... taxi stop
and boot it... *move move*...

D.

But in my somewhat utopian boy's club to argue as mature and complex our arrested state,* interest, always consensual, somehow persists in such growth. This might make us more sensitive is the custom.

in a philosophical sense the capacity of emotion or feeling, as distinguished from the intellect and the willy, which in popular use denotes a capacity of feeling of any kind, not merely hot or cold but sometimes a peculiar readiness to be the subject of feeling, and we so pray on our knees, on bended knees, especially the higher feelings of a person with a delicacy ready to be excited by the slightest cause, as displayed, for instance, in the "sensitive plant"...

*For so long the language describing our gay abandon was couched as an evolutionary negative; the heterosexual regime of dominance over women became the language regime over he who wants to be the bottom... in a manner of speaking.

"I'll be your bottom in the bedroom but I'll be good god-damned if I'm going to be your bottom outside that bedroom... Outside of the fucking inside of that stateless bedroom... is that straight enough?"

so long before you became aware, by yourself,
with the encouraging warmth of your flesh
enwrapped being, that every seat was taken,
and though there was very little standing room,
the back of the bus accommodated those will-
ing to deal with the exquisite discomfort...

"And how would you describe yourself in any
positive terms when even to get close to the
songs on the hit parade you'd have to change
the pronouns; if you had to do this just to iden-
tify yourself with the poetics of tin-pan alley,
what would you have to do when things got serious?"

d.

Georgie Porgy
puddin' an' pie
who doesn't like a slurp of puddin'
an' a wedge of pie?
Georgie Porgy
puddin' an' pie
blew the boys and made them cry
Ooo... puddin' an' pie...

E.

Of the ideal, relative maturity with rich mixtures, the other, the impurity of our practical affairs, a proper balance, a tacit consensus of a system, whatever the empirical evidence, that a massive agreement on fundamentals, the individual's highest faculties favour the open *ho-mo*genous, formed of parts that are all of the same kind: association incorporating misfit.

Highest type of excellence, ultimate object of attainment, actual or imaginary, may even be primal or slowly developed from failures and negations... the artist with his own mental image of which the completed work is an imperfect expression... the imaginary hitting smack dab into concrete

unable to carry a full load, trying to forget what memory knows, misplaced vocabulary, enlightenment of metaphor, dead lines, prose lines, the above lines... headlong in their own direction without me... their own truths I cannot claim... words I don't want to hear and having heard wonder how possibly could they be, their fascination already speaks, or why would they hold within themselves my fascination, my wonder... why is it they sound in other mouths, in other books, in other lines a weight and gravity beyond what I feel as my

adolescence... how is it they hook and I feel
their barbed tug... despite their limitations,
my deepening masturbations: consider
credulity...

e.

Credulity: the readiness to believe anything asserted as a fact merely because it is asserted; centrifugal slippage of the word in the twirling of spin...

the most paralysing form, the most efficient instrument of priestly domination: fear of the unknown, the foundation, the rock upon which it's built, from which grows faith in the power of the anointed to cast out fear... the fulcrum upon which the lever of religion rested...

did you say fulcrum... the divine fulcrum? We can't have that... use an altar boy, dogma style...

the more it apologizes, the more it tries to adjust to the observed facts, the more it appeals to experience and reason, the further it draws away from its pursuit by rack and thumbscrew, sword and flame, unable yet to give up its homo hunts in the coliseums of Christian sport...

F.

While neutral, a move towards political maturity with conflicting conditions for citizenship defines a still advertised multi-interest as singular interest concerned as a state engaged in one war... the kind Conservatives crave.

A falsehood might be a sudden unpremeditated statement... while a fabrication is a series of statements carefully studied and fitted together in order to deceive...

This was a get-together, not for the elected, but for the party: backroom guys, organizers, money men, some editors, and the PMO whole floors and their own dining room with one condition: Only one waiter, with us for the day, nobody else and he's discreet, got it? Discreet.

Told me over drinks one night, the drench of hatred in that room, they were anti everything, women, especially aboriginals, those god damned faggots, and those ragheads and slants, although we could use them, stoke up those religious views, their hardlines, set them off, "one agin' another, like... "

Tommy, my dear, you're looking pale...

f.

The Great War blew the lid off once and for all; elements of language blasted and burnt into near obliteration leaving in its wake the charred and shell-holed wasteland on which we were to re-speak. In the War of Fire, horror of hatred so humanly logical in its extension to the burning ovens, that it remainders us, gasping for words to face a nuclear fire that seared, in radioactivity, the gestures of burning humans on the few still standing walls in our heads...

take things to the limits and back off only because the powers get really scared about nowhere to go...

he realizes in longhand that it's not only what's put in but what's left out... another revision of his plans becomes necessary. the war is not over. it rages. with caution he withdraws his box cutter and begins to cut. it appears from the outside that someone is trying to get out...

G.

But for bringing into harmony, a nostalgia for small victims with intimations to resolution, is, on the contrary, that tension in this world preserved by politics expressed as: We are seeking to make the best of all possible for the already fully developed.

We had visions like sprinkles of pansy dust.

Not only lost, with its hope of being found, but totally forgotten in the deep quotidian; our self-driven immersion into trivia, diversions from the main event...

g.

It's easy to buy it, it's when you want another one exactly the same or something's gone wrong, and then the wall goes up about we've only got what they send us, we'd have to contact the warehouse or the distributor or the manufacturer or somebody inevitably out of reach, to make this the longest, most wasted lunch hour you've ever had and this is known so the staffer points to...

the SPECIAL!

... there was this guy, he worked on the floor at, I can't remember if it was a Zeller's or a Woolworths; it was on Bloor just west of Yonge, north side, he was big, a short guy gone fat, big round face in a red network of veins, a drinker, might have been gay or could have been, wearing on his large bald head a small white cowboy hat, looking so ridiculous I had to bury my face in a rack of shirts to hide my pained laughter, I'd forgotten it was WEST-ERN DAYS. What did he give up to be included in that retail community of meaning?

H.

Yet the case for form with ambiguous content becomes possible provided the population shares the important stress of style. That we required shared prescriptions of unavoidable scarcity to overcome both images of our childhood and its dictates...

An unfavourable connotation made or done on a whim, the use of choice words without special reference to thought expressed simply as the *vehicle* of thought, combinations somewhat technical with general dictions and limited wordings, the national speech employed makes up the clothing of thoughts in words, a range of words brought to display... style is the legal designation by which a person is known in official relations, a name born in infancy of one who does not have enough to live on with a total lack of material possessions, a state in which one must forego many of the necessities and all of the luxuries...

You would, late at night, if you were quiet enough, sneak out of bed, climb down from the top bunk, sliding back covers ever so carefully and twist around on your stomach and let your legs dangle over the edge of the mattress to reach down to touch the edge of the bunk below and step down where the

27

floorboards didn't creak. By gripping the doorknob to the bedroom door and slowly twisting it to the right and holding it when you heard the snick of the catch bolt release itself from the metal bolthole in the door jamb, pull the door to yourself slowly, very slowly, inching it back and releasing the door knob so you could step out of the bedroom. Avoiding the creaking floorboards just outside the doorway with a giant step you tip- toed across the rug to the kitchen door. If the door was slightly ajar you slid your fingers through the crack and gripped the door edge and lifted ever so slightly and firmly pulled the door open with the only noise being the swath of the door across the hideous brown-orange-ivory shag carpet. With the door open you would step onto the linoleum of the kitchen floor and tip- toe over to the fridge and with the tension of pushing it closed while pulling it open you could pop the fridge seal almost noiselessly, opening the door just a crack so as not to let the fridge light on and reach in to grab something to eat…

exhilarating arousal of snuck sex.

h.

All for the deep blunt awakening stab, my
morning juts in front outside of me, cuts the
air and strains (such a delicious strain) tension
that says I'm alive, I'm here, I'm empowered
and I've done it by myself, or better still, it's
done it by itself, its own head, the steaming
blood boner of it. turning point, axis of the
pole, so now what to do with it, keep the tension or pour it out, feel myself drain out into
the place I can put it this morning... how will
it take? can I take it? have it? do it? thrill in
the guts, quivering weak-kneed, tightening of
the ring, breath heavier, plummy weight of
stones where I can have anybody ending with
nobody. the slump after draining away and
the tempest this was for the minutes it took,
but not time, when in the middle there is only
it, the hand and the boner, the body, its now,
its demand to be appeased, dealt with beyond
the want of the mind's considerations ties ob-
ligations... take the shit shave shower and
shampoo to meet the almighty day.

I.

The deed had literary dedication given the black spot associated with its name. Should I amplify words on the invert? Such a procedure. I decided with all my limitations to understand what "I" meant. At recess I stayed behind, symbol to my regular confidant expectations, to then walk away with my black spot engaged into tears, rip-offs and disconnections...

One is never told about the cleanup... it's not shot for the money; it's not shot at all.

i.

Day breaks and is set waiting for what I could bring or the other way where the day brings possibilities I could respond to or catch. field the ball. how big is my mitt? it begins light grey but grows cold. it's unplanned and I am caught, out of doors without coat scarf or gloves. the cold seep. I go back to sit in the kitchen, get dinner ready, warm by the stove, preparing, cutting, small tasks to a known end. a late afternoon nap. my movement against the cold waiting behind the green, ready to blow itself into my room, under eaves through small cracks to stir and chill. a reminder it's always there, ready and waiting. it informs my view, my gathering, my economy, as I run between buildings and pockets of warmth to get around without having to meet it face to face like something you know about yourself...

J.

An ambiguous way deeply disturbed seemed plain. The more I thought who could have possibly demonstrated the simple fact that there could be no later, it was all now, I became acquainted...

I knew where it was, but not when it was, an introduction of a force; better still, an influence that unsettles or disarranges an orderly fixed course... while *boyish*, on the other hand, usually has entirely favourable implications; it describes the engaging or attractive qualities, "his trembling fineboned shoulder." *Boyish* may be said of girls, in reference to their clothes, looks, etc., and *girlish* of boys; the latter use connotes...

So who drew the line? Let's begin with one of the early ones breeding this discourse between women and men; she weaves at home while he sails off for action in exotic lands...

Right now in this present read any want ads for Men on Women, Women on Men, Women on Women and Men on Men, (how else could it be?), and read the classified ad menus to find that phrase we've inherited through some thousands of years: "Wanted: Greek Action." And you're telling me in all those words and

adventures, Ulysses never met one homosexual
Greek...

C'mon... ?

j.

I took my sailor's physical last week. The doctor removed some blood from my arm, which made the guy behind me turn pale in the grip of epic forces. I didn't mind the blood test so much, but the eye test worried me. Sailors expect 20-20 vision of a chart reader. Luckily, I was able to read every line. Afterwards, Tommy, who'd turned pale, went with me to get some... nautically speaking.

K.

I found myself in trouble as a child... my somewhat personal distinction between two principles of association, where an association is formal rules of duty, where my childhood, by my dedication at least, needed no rule...

An unenviable position, the project then, was to make it enviable by strategies: how to have your cake and eat it too... not always possible, best place to start campaigning though...

k.

Fear of: starvation, being eaten, being poi-
soned, being choked, being chopped to pieces,
being drowned, being castrated,
being dropped...

"its source is constituted by various erogenous
zones which acquire psychic dominance according to a pre-programmed epigenetic schedule... "

a schedule of becoming, in one's individual
fashion, aware of one's body and what it does
as you begin to find out it's you...

nose hole connected to the mouth hole
mouth hole connected to the asshole
asshole connected to the brain stem
brain stem connected to the head brain

dem holes   dem holes   dem hot holes
dem holes in de face of de cold

"Did I tell you warmth is key?"

L.

A formalization of the group too high a price to pay for an association formally. The strongest element itself a belief in the efficacy that the faint of heart (myself) considered speaking in the first place. Mark my first principle of the word "aspiration", which would unite, by a shared recognition of interests, my rites of passage, the occasion of an ambitious breath.

"Huge negativities grafted onto my identity... by whom? that somehow by taking it giving it letting him take the wide open intimacy (a mutual by our understanding) was somehow demeaning making you less   for something not only they didn't know but seemed to be afraid of... those straight ones to whom i got close so very close i became aware... by myself with the encouraging warmth of my flesh-enwrapped being... warmth is key."

1.

They met when one was 9 and the other 10 and here they were at 24 and 25, things heading in different directions. I'd seen one of them while sitting in Allen Gardens. He walked up the diagonal path from Jarvis Street and I watched him walk this way, with his coat over his shoulder. He saw me on the bench, I waved him over, he sat down. I asked how he was doing... he turned and leaned up towards me, as he'd been slouched, elbows on knees... his eyes, the level of tears before he squelched, and they slid... "We're splitting up... "

M.

One party, clearing in the woods, comes out to a safe distance. The other offering what may be ultimately consummated without hostilities being risked, remained. Close proximity with one and possible success of such willingness to accept the rules of the game makes it clear; I do not mean to impart there cannot be rules until I make my peace with him, as I am using him, I mean... the forest for the trees.

To embody in fact what was before in thought, doing the utmost that is necessary to make fact all that is done but limited quite sharply to the concluding act, the money paid, the goods delivered, finishing as a whole with approaches to perfection.

m.

"You could choose a drawing or drawings directly. We've obtained a sketchbook and are now showing it to those regular clients with a discerning eye interested in acquiring depth in this artist. Besides, relatively speaking, they're quite inexpensive."

Told to as many clients as there were sketches; the selection from one to another completely changing as sketches were removed... the comparisons from the first purchases, in most cases from an untrained but acquisitive eye, the most obvious coloured drawings were taken. It would, by process of sale and elimination, destroy the sketchbook and its interrelated narrative of lines as the sketchbook was destroyed, in a singular twist of irony, the drawings, no matter how sketchy, improved in their now scanty comparisons.

You buy when you see the drawing and if later you desire beyond it, as your knowledge and taste have grown, or further understanding of your own likes and dislikes, you can pursue this by selling the "younger one," and by whatever means someone in a similar financial arena as you were when you bought it has their eyes light up at what they've found, as you move closer to your own person as by this painting

sending its signal which for some reason you
in particular are picking up; it's doing that for
everybody, but you own it...

N.

Allowed to enter and hold his in the law. Reports,
literally church quarrels, in the books. The courts
have disputes, first views of a shared commitment.
Who holds open the door to the most faithful
opposing formal rules? Access to internal law.

*"this isn't about chapter and verse not about rote
but about   thinking"*

An intensity commonly involving sharpness of
feeling and sometimes acrimony or anger, being
less methodical or orderly than a debate...

I often visit the root cellar where the votive can-
dles flicker in the draft of my arrival to pay *hom-
age*, to massage my regrets, to thank my lucky
stars I'm gay. I've noticed a pattern of abandonment; a leaving behind of those who loved me
as I felt, albeit deeply disguised as arrogance,
unworthy. I had awoken with a dream, livid in
this dull morning, of juggling, so muscle-sore,
so fatigued in both body and spirit, I could no
longer juggle to keep the balls up and wanting,
desperately, for somebody to recognize this and
lend a hand while knowing I could not ask. I
could no longer keep up my façade of compe-
tence; no longer take my place at my seemingly
allotted table in the flea market, knowing I was
nothing but a peddler of the broken the chipped

and the incomplete. It was I who turned or ran away, losing touch with what I now know as losing both them and myself; not bothering in my self-inflicted focus. I've spent so much time alone among others I've learned to blow on my own coal to keep darkness at bay and warmth close. I've maintained a niche where the votives glow; a place on the ladder of my time where I can ascend amoebafishreptilepro-mammalape-*homo*-sapiens or descend at will, prompted by a piece of music, a jog of memory, to visit the root cellar devoted to my time. A hole in the ground without god or gods but my own who've inhabited this space since my first breath, who will sit with me to nudge me, cajole me, goad and remind me of the moment I walked their straight line drawn in some righteous quicksand that in its very drawing one is made to slip, and, covered in muck be pointed out as one of the unclean; or washed, be absolved, be brought into the fold, the whole setup constructed so one doesn't have to make choices but rather take the word of an anointed; the sound of his foot-steps coming down the row of beds at night armed and hard with his moral choices. I lay curled, without god or gods to enfold me, to spin in this great blackness, my seedling in a crumble of my own significant soil pushes forth my pale tendrilous horn...

(with apologies to Theodore Roethke)

A Touchy Subject

On one side, God made our arms long enough to touch it.
On the other, we evolved arm length so we could touch it.
So, no matter which way you argue you can still touch it.

n.

An exhaustion of our ability to have a religious experience; not that the equipment is rusted, or a glitch, or a brown-out, but a completely scorched impetus towards that experience burdened as it is by utter disbelief in its language of guilt...

poured out generation after generation to be filed in the catacombs of dead books, theological corpses eternally unreadable, completely dead, not so much from their manifest errors but their utter uselessness; not one grain to the sum of human knowing, but our submission and their domination... not how many dance on the head, but with the sharp end who gets pricked?

"Hear the one about the Irish homo... ?"

"Bless me Father, for I have sinned... it's been weeks since my last confession.
Is that you Michael?
Aye, Father, 'tis.
And what have you been up to, me son?
I've been havin' sexual relations... with another man.
With another man, you say...
Aye, Father.
Not Darcy down by the Kilkenny Road?

Oh no, Father, I don't want to be namin'
names.
Was it Patrick from the old town?
Oh no, Father, I don't want to be namin'
names, I'm just here for the atonement.
Little Johnny from over by the river?
Oh no, Father, just the atonement.
Well, Michael, we'll have no more of these
sins against Nature and that'll be five Our
Fathers, four Hail Marys and see that you stick
to the straight and narrow.
Aye, Father.

He leaves the confessional and goes to do his
penance where his friend Sean is sitting and
waiting.

Michael, what did you get?

Five Our Fathers,
Four Hail Marys and
Three good leads."

O.

On the surface, the simplest principle of affairs,
of what matters, is affected by a formal vote; a
member being done in is inevitably involved.
Suppose a vote by the government to convert
every kind of member; the voter holds but
small limits on the government's uncomfortable govern-mental doctrine:

to suppose is temporarily to assume a thing as
true, either with the expectation of finding it
so or for the purpose of ascertaining what
would follow if it were so.

To suppose is also to think a thing to be true
while aware or conceding that the belief does
not rest upon any sure ground, and may not
accord with fact; or yet again, to suppose is to
imply as true or involved as a necessary infer-
ence; window dressing supposes the existence
of a window dresser:

Window shopping modelled on prescriptions
of pose, glass barriers between lookers and
looked-at, continual display of enactment hung
in the balance but very much on offer...

need suggests the possibility of supplying the
deficiency that want expresses...

"I need a winter coat,
I want fur… "

condition of one who does not have enough
to live on.

0.

On the government's uncomfortable govern-
mental doctrine: Kleptomania!

"not unto my cleave you don't!"…

but after the joke, getting serious with, let me
see… how about parenting; do you get what
you raise, not what you breed?

P.

This disposition of mind by theory of identity and the multitude orally neutral is the standard applicable to institutional roles. The cop on the corner with a strange taboo concerning personal discharge...

To free from something imposed by others, to take out of the hands of others, free from so-called legal restraint. A price, however, is always demanded: we finish a letter, complete a lifework, consummate a bargain, effect a purpose, execute a command, fulfil a promise, perform our daily tasks, realize an ideal, accomplish a design, achieve a victory... own a standing in law.

p.

If I hadn't known by the open closet door I'd
have known by the trail of burnt matches trail-
ing the length of the hallway that we'd been
robbed. I couldn't at first find what had been
taken; the electronics were all in their places
but in the kitchen the cupboards were open,
along with the drawer at the bottom of the
stove. Canned goods were missing from the
stacks of tuna and soup. The bread was gone,
which somehow prompted me to look in the
fridge, and gone were the cold cuts and some
veggies. Toothpaste, some rather expensive
cologne, and a bottle of mouthwash no longer
in the bathroom. In the bedroom they'd taken
Billy's leather pants and a jacket; was he going
to be pissed or what?

I phoned the landlord, who insisted I call the
cops and report it so there would be an incident number to use on the insurance claim.
While on the phone I noticed the linen cup-
board door was also ajar, and peered in, while
the landlord protested at my description of his
back door locks as shit. Goddammit, one
towel out of each set had been stolen... Billy
was gonna be real upset because nothing would
match... yeah, yeah, I'll call the police.

I told them about the B&E and gave my work address and I could take the officer down the street to the apartment when he arrived which he did a day later… an older guy with ginger hair and a reddening complexion after huffing up the stairs. I took him through the events, about being out to dinner and coming home and finding what I'd found, while he wrote in his notebook. He wandered around and asked if I lived alone. No, I live here with my partner. "Your partner?" "Yeah." He wrote it in his notebook. I wondered if he was going to lick his pencil. We finished up with him saying there had been a number of B&E's in the area because of the rat's nest of apartments over in the next block and then he left.

Billy, back from cottage country, despite my having phoned on burglary night, wanted all the details, so I walked him through it and we discovered why the oven drawer had been left open: pots were missing. We laughed about the burglar needing stuff for a dinner date he was hosting.

"You fucking lied to me and you were up here with somebody behind my back you can't be trusted with shit while I'm away for one whole fucking week and you can't handle… "

"What're you talking about?"

"That cop came here this morning said he had to tidy things up and told me you had some goddamn trick in here and you gave him every-thing... "

"I gave him everything... he fucking said that... the cop... "

Reassure him? It took weeks while

TO SERVE AND PROTECT

sniggered in the locker room, "You shoulda heard how I set those fags up... "

Q.

A familiar case of self-perpetuating inward-turning duty voluntarily commanding as applied to the injunction "thou shall not kill a man's talents." Would his fellows ask, "How?"

Generally so abused, especially as the requirement by legal authority that certain actions be suspended or refrained from, pending final legal decisions defining order and direction; sailors simply have to obey the nature of things as in specific requirements of the position...

Disposition of the limbs of the body in a particular way; a reclining posture or an erect posture; while attitude is the position appropriate to the expression of some feeling consciously assumed in an attempt to propose a yarn (originally nautical slang), a long rambling tale of adventure and travel of doubtful truth and seldom having a clear plot.

9.

Yeah, give me some cheap, yeah cheap, I like
it cheap, put it in cheap, deeper cheap yeah
cheap up there cheap faster cheap deeper cheap
give it to me cheap I want it cheap   o yeah
cheap fulfilling cheap hot cheap real cheap
good cheap o yeah cheap cheaper cheapest
good 'n' cheap...

R.

In the normal course toward dominance, some crisis brings to life a new form, which, once under way, feeds on itself and only seems to sink out of sight...

That was the lie right there, it didn't feed on itself, it fed itself on us; the disguise was necessary what with the dawning truth of our expendability firmly established as a kind of fullness in the constructed vacuum of our narrative- trained mind...

"Unholy stiffies, Gayman, look!

What's up, Butt Boy... ?

There's a beginning, and over there a middle and, Makin' Whoopee, Gayman, there's an ending... ! Dollars to doughnuts and my giddy uncle, something's up... "

Beelzebub's bum, Butt boy, I think you're right... There! A novel's running down the up escalator!"

But what if the plot didn't have a narrative that commonly connotes fact rather than fiction, while anecdote tells briefly some incident assumed to be fact only if it passes close limits of brevity... the story as quickie nearly synonymous with tale used for the imaginative, the legendary, especially of ancient date; a fairy tale.

AIDS was a big leveller. The whole freedom to have with another man where it could be just that, the verb, was completely out of the bounds of anything remotely corporate, knowing full well its root in *corpus*, the body. We only needed another. Sex of the first remove having to wrap it; latex not friendly to soft tissue, so expensive price fixed water-borne lubes to facilitate, where, tripping over to Allen Gardens deep in the bushes the night air cool on your body sliding over you his warm hand and we would... with kisses and appreciations go on our way with no price on what we'd made; until squeezed into brackets with all that so-called disposable income, the outgo, we left behind, but retained in ancient body memory: the in out come go...

r.

Constituted by various "erogenous zones" which acquire psychic dominance according to a pre-programmed epigenetic schedule...

you found a place of such sensation, such thrill and warmth that after finding it you went back finding not only the place but how to get there, over and over...

your growing sense of your own body; its pathways...

all of the fear is of this fact: that we're here as body, here now slipping on ice, spilling coffee, knee-capping somebody with a briefcase... getting from A to B in your body... realizing late, it's a wet one,   a sneeze with a mouthful, where *do* you put your food shrapnelled and saliva glazed palm, whip-lash of a snot string on the side of your nose... betrayed by your body...

your legs back, she washed the beauty of your little round bum with a warm wet cloth   the heat the softness   the love within her caress...

"His so soft little face and him at my nipple... I pull it out sometimes and splash his face and lick him clean... his so soft skin, his baby smell tasting of my milk."

... to later reproduce that over and over, slightly different each and every time, unlike some gadget assembly-lined...

you'd learned to do it by yourself, now you were learning with someone else.

S.

An association newly formed of shared commitment, for some time of heart, will not stop for those strong in spirit. But as time goes, less obvious is the backsliding possibility which prospers, as in the case of a demand. Plainly, wills testing conditions toward overt change, dispute.

How much were we supposed to absorb, how many more burdens were we to heft into our backpack, yet one more wafer of humiliation, another dehydrated snack pack while we so generously accepted the heft of religious intolerance built on our backs. Were the societies in which we found ourselves so fragile as to be endangered by allowing our perspective, our sexual proficiency? Those places in a vast life become communities of meaning where our behaviour over all time becomes, at last, identity.

I'll dispense with the prologue whose sole purpose is to assuage the inbred guilt about, not just doing it, but doing it alone. Wanting, exactly, to be alone, but to be above all, safely alone. This means there is no possibility of ever being seen or caught, caught with your pants down... nothing worse than being with the urge and no place to indulge.

So I sat them down, looked straight into their faces, and told them to fuck off, and those feelings of self-loathing...

they fucked off.

s.

It wasn't as if I'd been trained in the pleasure palaces of the Far East or anything... I was looking for love in the only places I'd ever received some attention, if only I could please him...

T.

In modern terms the relevant exile is naturally self-imposed; an occasion entitled to be ordinarily controlled, of humankind as number...

to call by name a delicate balance between coming and going... held for as long as possible to take time out of time within content... to lift out... to gather something in the interim... an outside influence subdued... a relaxation of distrust...

as for the salesman who would use art to gain some soul; artists respond by sabotaging the links, allowing chaos... a plot misplaced by culture... culture credible only as it pertains to gardening, cultivation of a sensitive plant, acculturation upon which reputations are built, valid only as we say yes... authority being investment in belief... so barf a pinch of ink in that direction and proceed into that orifice of particular formal content... those who derive their form systems righteously punish severely... so straight ahead with a few bends to keep up the metaphor... but not deviation.

"Humph ... a likely story!"

t.

They forgot the stamps... they forgot the
fuckin' stamps for the invites but the place
filled up with grey flannels that retail for $145
a pair. they said hang it in the window. people
would look at it from the street like beefsteak.
and there you go, they were taking the scumble
and asking for more. and saying to your
brother that it was all right. he weaving pissed
out of shape saying this. the audience listening
with wine and creamy brie slipping down
crackers. wheat crackers. they were talking
about the painting the way women say men
in locker rooms talk about their length.   no
question of what do you and i and the afternoon spent on your couch and the languid
bitch you really are and your oriental maid
and her serving and the beer you poured on
your ink drawings and the jokes about going
up your ass and the delicious twat it really
was. you were leaking gold and crimson down
your pant leg and we swallowed the perform-
ance whole and begged for more and that languid bitch Domino, o holy buns, sylph
adorned baby, gave us green and not one colour
but the mixture of ochre and blue plus red
and brown and what happened when the light
struck from the west window and the drying,
the seco, the pintura, standing to be framed,
his chin posed with a resolute bright painting

and the expression of price and what was the
art but not price, no price but for the left after...

U.

The point which I have illustrated at the height of this administration's obscenities have determined: crisis is upon "them"...

decisive turn, turning point, and yes, critical juncture culminating in a balancing act between opportunity and danger... the reach to grasp a coveted thing... embarrassing when you're out there alone, but if you do it together in a community of expertise you can circle the wagons to build the ramparts between us and them...

a regime that is governed more by broad principles than specific rules...

"A prescriptive, rules-based regime that provides for a significant degree of day-to- day supervision by regulators could inadvertently create the perception that such approval and their ratings are 'fail-proof' because they have a regulatory 'seal of approval',   said the regime...

only one thing to be asked then: "what exactly are your present and future broad principles," not that we should take anything from the past into account; like pyramids and their schemes...

u.

Thy kingdom come just came, mortar of its granite walls powdering into sand scouring at the wind's edge over trenches of mud, blood, and brain matter. (O, aye matey to larboard and starboard and before the wind on the good ship *Codswallop*) sand blasting across the Empire and here's the thing; we need fodder lots and lots of fodder, and they gave us a parade to the station and lit fireworks in a version of what was to come over there, this is radio free, star shells lighting up no man's land, hideous drift of bloat flesh caught in fencing wire like rag dolls and rubbish, horses tangled in the wagon wrecks, rictus of their lips, stiff like snorkels in sea shit and body parts, wind drift howling...

... another hour before the hunk of grey bread swiped in bacon grease with a tin of pale bitter tea to wash it down, along with raw onions we devour like apples...

... run past that hollow in the wall of mortar and gunfire where the voice of one of your mates with his legs blown off pleads not to be left and you run on to get past that hollow and the hollow in yourself, running and slipping in the blood mixed muck...

language, burnt and pock-marked with Lewis-gun fire, gutted by bayonets that get caught and won't come unstuck until the rifle is fired, legs blown off at the knee and still for a few seconds running back to our trenches like death sentences on blood squelching trunks grabbing at the heels of passing comrades...

the beak-nosed spectre that haunts November...

V.

Shifts from the act to the mind have done
something against formal rules. I can understand it has always had that side to it, a kind
of attitude. Indeed, in the other extreme, when
as juror in judgement there is a conscious effort
toward the act: a citizen unable to respond at
the other end of his mind...

We weren't any part of that, the way heteros
had kids and then deserted them, or daddies
who played your nipples with a fork, no, we
homos did unto our Others as we did unto
ourselves: turned the other cheek... not that
we didn't have our fair share of blonde bombers
and complete screw-ups, we played unto ourselves and never bent to the edifice built on
heterosexual backs...

in those shimmering towers, his finger put
down on you and your identity gone in the
place where behind the text is the backroom
door with special keys and hidden faces who
know too much, who as yet have not worked
out that there're other doors on down this hallway of mirrors
                    of mirrors

v.

What if, on the ladder of your ascent, you
stopped? what if on the ladder of your ascent
you had been so wounded as to be unable to
climb, almost stunted but for that small part
of yourself, while stopped and unable, turned
to look into backward infinity... to ask...

not, who am i? not, how was i made but why
do i like the sex i like..?

W.

The notion that our basic disposition towards any person indicates an "act" we should remember interventions are actually brought through play. The act serves largely. It is an accident of vital processes of effective public scrutiny only seemingly guaranteed.

The play's the thing, a powerful element of play and game to generate multipliers, complications to layer the course for the normal elements of human communication; something lost, almost forgotten, buried by the manufactured separations of the deep quotidian...

perception of the unusual, the commonly unperceived, quite likely relations between the apparently unrelated, said to depend upon a union of surprise and pleasure.

w.

Slip a straw into it, the way you would a straw in a milkshake, not one of those thin chemical ones, but an old-fashioned one with real cream. watch the way it folds around the straw, a lip where it enters the shake, moving up the inside of the straw as it slips in. draw on it until the back of your head caves in.

The fire is out. men from Station #9 came, fought and left leaving four walls, a collapsed roof and a charred interior. blown out windows show black in an otherwise flawless exterior.

Sifting through the remains, Chief Fire Inspector Hamilton's province is melted fragments, collapsed faces of charred dolls, melded synthetic bed covers, black brass buttons, and half-burnt shoes. placing all these things on an elaborate mesh screen he sifts them until a small hill of pure black soot is formed. on a pocket- sized glass plate he chops soot and snorts it through a straw. he reports he can better apprehend causes...

X.

Reform has been a total abandonment of television. Unintimidated intimate association enjoyed without government.

So what we want, right at the moment where plot climbs to an emotional peak just before the apex to splice without warning, a kind of suspended *coitus interruptis* smoothed out so the money shot is our product placement, square in every watcher's eyeball... can we also raise up the decibel level and do that for the internet like we did for TV... yeah, can we do that?

I just wanna slide right in there with you right up next to the slide you really really want...

X.

Don't we just slide ourselves in, so much easier if agreed upon a particular carrot, don't you think? Well, yes, the sign said Lettuce and Tomatoes go together; the Tomato you get depends on the Lettuce you have. So, yes, that is one pursuit, a fashionable suit that posing wears them all but only some last which begs even more inquiry, how they weigh, a relation not so everlasting, and how were they fore and aft of not so lasting, seemingly in need to be between, an intervention by one in the affairs of another.

Can we take that last one... as an instance? One may suppose, but so many directions to pick. So which one? Anyone of your choosing. Just stab at one? Yes. But you told me before the interview you were to choose one and I would respond as that's where I excel and now you've changed it. I felt we were on a flow only to be interrupted by a change I didn't want to come between us.

Oh!

Some thousands of hits per day, taking us by giving us what we want but can't have... the rehearsed extension into the hyper-real, beyond idealistic, into the unattainable, while driving madly beyond our quotidian...

Y.

Of other associations the balance is delicate.
We should recall the range of disparate members of varying disciplines and hardships, conditions apt to be forgotten when talking right
becomes as important as acting right.

Quite delicate because this is the inheritance
of language and its coagulation in the group
you were born into beyond the wordplay of
mother tongue. Remembering one and another one in a conjunction, as if that was the
only con... Join, they said, and without 20-
20 or hindsight unable to discern the pattern
occupied by the loan; to embody, to form one
body so trippingly gay, or the prince of mas-
turbation?

Note the "either/or" of the incomplete conjunction.

y.

City shadows in the canyons of commerce
were cool, light moving from shade to brighter
as I crossed the street into full sun where the
woman, slightly buckled at the knees, juddered
stiff-armed, while her shaking head flung foam
into the air, quiet but for the granny dressed
in black running in circles, waving scrawny
limp-skinned arms over her head while she
wailed.

A middle aged woman running out of the
Wander Hotel accosts me; she has no shoes or
teeth; for eight dollars she'll give me a blow
job... she says she's clean.

A pair of legs dangling from the rump of somebody bent over the rim of an apartment block
garbage bin.

A young girl in a print dress wearing low heeled
shoes and talking to herself wanders the halls
of an apartment building in which she doesn't
live.

It was hot... towers shimmering and silent
but for these infirm human oases I quickly
skirted...

Z.

May a man not feel who knows he may later be considered unsuited to both sides? A nightmare world in which he declares only, "O boy, did I get enough..?"

I saw him tonight. I was feeling house bound and sweaty. I needed to go out so took Spot for a late-night walk. Bumped into him over by Livingstone Park, going to work. He's smoothed himself with pancake, dyed himself blonde and gelled it upward in a young cut so when the headlights slow down he could step out of the entranceways into the streetlight looking good for their good look, their first impression, and would in that instant know if the fantasy was right. Was he right? Was he young under the streetlight, the spotlight?

"I've been doin' real good, a thousand every coupla nights. Yeah, it's beyond all that abuse stuff now and I'm likin' it. I'm gonna move into a two-bedroom in the Eastend. Craig, he's a real hunk."

He gets all huggy and a bit girly at this, arms wrapping himself and turning this way and that, happy. He lights up, offers a toke.

"What ya doin' with the money?" I don't let him answer and jump right in with... "You gotta put some away; you need a safe hidey-hole."

"I got one, I really got one, she's old, she's sixty and I bring her stuff and she has it. She counts it out."

"She's not going to use it? She croaks and who's to say it's yours?
It's gotta be secure. You'll need it because too soon too old."

"Okokaay. I'll call ya, love ya."

"Yeah, yeah... "

"For some people their entire lives are about sex. They're steam valves and whistle when we want. When we want. They're there, outside who or what you bring home. Outside your home. They have seen and they have done and they make us afraid for what we have done when we see them and we put them. Put them down. We know what they do and what we want, really really want."

z.

This book also relates how it's been made and from which word events it sprang along with the "story," if you will.   A reader follows by reading the creative chain to whatever end. Winning books omit how what you're reading was made to allow you an untroubled passive unthinking experience... This does not!

That's not to say I don't want an untroubled passive unthinking experience of sex, action, and travel to exotic lands every now and then. I just find I can't consume like I used to. I'm busy practising being *no one*, like Odysseus.

USED BOOKS USED
IN THE MAKING OF THIS BOOK

VOLUNTARY ASSOCIATIONS, edited by J. Roland Pennock & John W. Chapman, Atherton Press, New York, 1969.

SYNONYMS, ANTONYMS, and PREPOSITIONS, James C. Fernald, LHD, Funk & Wagnalls, New York, 1947, revised.

The NATURAL HISTORY OF EVIL, Adam Gowans Whyte, Watts & Co., London, 1920.

GENERALS DIE IN BED, Charles Yale Harrison, Potlatch Publications Limited, sixth printing, 1995.

PROLOGUE

If you believe the notion that we all have content searching for form, then the only assailant is silence, and if you own such silence, and know it, then a trigger can break it. Ascribing to the idea that writing is informed by reading, the simple book-loving act of picking through a table of used books is the beginning of *A Few Sharp Sticks*. What bpNichol described as a "book hit" occurred when I found a book of essays concerning political and legal philosophy pertaining to, and titled, *Voluntary Associations*.

Thinking that most of what we engage in is voluntary association, I read through the book, taking note of the triggers while selecting and collapsing sentences and paragraphs into what I refer to as "kernels." I selected twenty-six, and lettered them from A to Z, thinking the alphabet more neutral than a numbering which could give the impression of a hierarchy of value not intended. Building on these kernels by selecting key words, and defining them by employing the same selective process applied in the kernel selections, using *Funk & Wagnalls Standard Handbook of Synonyms Antonyms & Prepositions*, I generated definitions into which I infused gay biography sharpened with pointed questions, jokes, hypocritical religiosity, literary assumptions, art ownership and gay life descriptions for heterosexual readers. (O butch it up, Mary, of course I include gay readers.) I've never wanted to write cock and ball stories, but am rather more interested in writing about a different thinking mind in a different thinking brain: A way of seeing through the lens of gay sensibility where, in society at large, the unasked and unanswered question, "Did you choose your hetero-sexuality?" gets a thorough prodding, along with some "fluffy red hearts." However, with the silence broken, the writing didn't feel complete, so I proceeded to write to what was already written by adding further comment. The "new" writing were addenda occasioned by the writing in the already alphabetized upper case sections and defined by using the lower case. The best of it was the fact the lower case sections don't always follow logically but are, by intention, associative.

Your reading is your writing, is among the many things bp taught me. I have content and the reading only supports it, gives it a voice, or better still gives words, descriptions, confirmations and outright disagreements until form is found. A way in, a kind of sorting of what you know and what, as a writer, I need to say to break silence.

83